Elizabeth against a bully . . .

"Thanks for waiting, Elizabeth. Go ahead and take the paper back to Mrs. Otis." Miss Johnson turned around and began writing some long math problems on the board.

I reached for the sign-up sheet. Patty held it out with a smirk. Then she dropped the paper onto the floor. When I bent down to pick it up, she stepped on my fingers. It was no accident! I looked at Miss Johnson. She was still writing on the board.

"Go ahead. Pick it up," whispered Patty.

I rubbed my fingers. They hurt!

"Are you afraid of a piece of paper?" Patty hissed. "What a scaredy-cat."

Bantam Books in the SWEET VALLEY KIDS series

SWEET VALLEY KIDS

SCAREDY-CAT ELIZABETH

Written by
Molly Mia Stewart

Created by
FRANCINE PASCAL

Illustrated by
Ying-Hwa Hu

BANTAM BOOKS
NEW YORK·TORONTO·LONDON·SYDNEY·AUCKLAND

RL 2, 005-008

SCAREDY-CAT ELIZABETH
A Bantam Book / September 1995

*Sweet Valley High® and Sweet Valley Kids® are
registered trademarks of Francine Pascal*

Conceived by Francine Pascal

*Produced by Daniel Weiss Associates, Inc.
33 West 17th Street
New York, NY 10011*

Cover art by Susan Tang

ISBN: 0-553-48213-0

Published simultaneously in the United States and Canada

*Bantam Books are published by Bantam Books, a division of Bantam
Doubleday Dell Publishing Group, Inc. Its trademark, consisting of the
words "Bantam Books" and the portrayal of a rooster, is Registered in the
U.S. Patent and Trademark Office and in other countries. Marca
Registrada. Bantam Books, 1540 Broadway, New York, New York 10036.*

PRINTED IN THE UNITED STATES OF AMERICA

OPM   0 9 8 7 6 5 4 3 2 1

*To Ada Szeto and
Michael Rubin*

CHAPTER 1

Bad News on the Bus

"Jess, hurry up! We'll be late for the bus." I stood by the front door, waiting for my sister.

"I'll be there in a minute." Jessica peeked her head over the top of the stairs. "I can't get my ponytail right." She disappeared again.

I'm Elizabeth Wakefield, and Jessica is my identical twin. That means it's really hard to tell us apart. We both have long blond hair and blue-green eyes. Mom and Dad and our big brother, Steven, can tell who is who. Well, most of the time. We wear name bracelets so other people don't get us mixed up. Sometimes, though, it's fun to switch bracelets and trick our friends!

Even though we look alike, Jessica and I are as different as salt and pepper. She likes to play with dolls and wear fancy dresses. I'd rather play tag or read a book by my favorite author, Angela Daley.

We're different at school, too. Even though we sit next to each other in our second-grade class at Sweet Valley Elementary, we never act like each other. Jessica's favorite things about school are lunch and recess. That's when she plays "princesses" with her friends Lila Fowler and Ellen Riteman. *My* favorite thing about school is learning! At recess I usually play soccer with my friends Todd Wilkins and Amy Sutton.

But there is one thing Jessica and I agree about—our teacher, Mrs. Otis.

She's the most super teacher in the whole world! All the kids in our class love her.

Yesterday Mrs. Otis announced that she was organizing a science fair at school. I was so excited! Anybody could enter, as long as they could get a display ready by the end of the next school week. The science fair was going to be on Friday night, so parents could come.

I wanted Jessica to be my partner. We do everything together. But when I asked her, she made a face. "Yuck, science!" she said.

Luckily, Amy Sutton and Julie Porter said they wanted to be in the science fair, too. So now the three of us are a team! We planned to have the best exhibit in the school.

"Jess!" I called again. My sister never worried about being late. I was tired of waiting, so I went outside to watch for the bus. I thought about ideas for the

3

science fair. Andy Franklin was doing a volcano. Kisho Murasaki and Todd Wilkins were making something called a tornado tube. Two third-grade girls planned to make electricity with a potato. It seemed as if all the interesting ideas were taken. What could Julie, Amy, and I do?

I leaned against a tree near the driveway. A spider was spinning a web in the branches just above me. I watched it swing back and forth, making a beautiful design out of silvery thread. I forgot all about going to school.

"Liz! The bus is coming! Hurry up!" Jessica called. I jumped and grabbed my book bag.

" 'Bye, Mr. Spider. Thanks for your help!" I jogged toward Jessica and the other kids waiting at the bus stop. I couldn't wait to get to school!

"What's the big smile for?" asked Jessica.

4

"I have the perfect idea for my science-fair project."

"What is it?" she asked.

"I can't tell you. Not before I tell Amy and Julie," I answered. The bus arrived and we lined up to get on.

"That's not fair!" Jessica followed me up the bus steps. "We're twins. We tell each other everything!"

I pretended to zip my lip. Jessica hated not knowing secrets. This was going to drive her buggy!

I was still giggling when I got onto the bus. I started down the aisle to our regular seat. Then I gasped. There was somebody else sitting in our spot!

It was a girl I didn't know. A big girl with short brown hair. I guessed that she was new to our school. She probably didn't know that Jessica and I sat in that seat every day.

"Hi," I said in my friendliest voice. "I'm Elizabeth Wakefield. You must be new."

5

The girl didn't say anything.

"You probably didn't know, but this is where Jessica and I sit every day," I explained. "We're twins, and we always sit together."

The girl still didn't say a word.

"Do you think you could move back a seat, maybe? I mean, we always sit in this seat." I smiled.

The girl didn't smile back. She just kept looking at me.

"Take your seats, girls," the bus driver called.

I stepped back so the new girl could move to another seat.

She didn't move.

"You could sit back there by Crystal," I suggested. "She's really nice."

"Why don't you sit back there by Crystal?" the girl snapped. She gave me a crabby look. "I don't see your name on this seat. And I don't take orders from shrimpy little kids like you."

6

She spread her stuff all over our seat. "What are you going to do about it, Elizabeth Wakefield?"

I looked at the girl. She was big and she looked tough. I knew just what I was going to do about it.

I took Jessica's hand and we moved back to a different seat.

The new girl's loud, mean laugh echoed through the whole school bus.

CHAPTER 2
Going Buggy

"Our seat is more comfy," Jessica complained as we sat down.

"I kind of like the view from back here," I said. "It's good to try sitting someplace different, once in a while."

Jessica brushed her bangs back off her face. "I wouldn't mind if it was *my* idea to sit here. I don't like that new girl bossing us around."

"I don't either. But we can have fun together wherever we sit. Right?"

That made Jessica smile. "Right. Now, tell me what your idea is for the science fair."

"Nope! Not until I tell Amy and Julie." I got out my math book. "Come on. Let's study for our math test."

Jessica wrinkled her nose. "We studied so hard last night, I even dreamed about subtraction!" She closed my book. "Let's play a game. I know! I'll try to guess what you thought of for the science fair. How's that?"

I smiled. Jessica couldn't stand not knowing other people's secrets. "OK," I said. "You get twenty guesses."

She was on guess number nineteen when we got to school.

"Is it about solar power?" she asked.

"No," I said. "And that's twenty."

"You have to tell me!" she begged. We moved into the aisle to get off the bus.

"I promise I will. *After* I tell Amy and Julie." I started down the aisle.

Suddenly Jessica grabbed my arm. "Let *her* get off first," she whispered, pointing at the new girl.

10

"Good idea," I said. We let Todd and some other kids go by, and then we got off the bus. I looked around but didn't see that new girl anywhere. I did see Lila Fowler and Ellen Riteman. They were waving to Jessica.

"Jess! Come here!" they called to her. Jessica skipped happily over to her friends, forgetting all about guessing my secret.

As I started walking toward the school, I saw that new girl watching me. The look she gave me made me shiver.

"Hi, Elizabeth." Amy and Julie came running up.

The new girl disappeared into the crowd of kids.

"Are you OK?" asked Amy. "You don't look very happy."

"I'm OK," I said. "It's just that I met a new girl on the bus who wasn't very nice." I told them about what had happened. "I tried to be polite when I told

11

her she was in our seat. She just took it all wrong."

"I hope she doesn't end up in *our* class," said Amy.

"She's too big to be a second-grader," I said.

"Maybe she was nervous about starting at a new school," suggested Julie.

"I don't know," I said. "She seemed more mean than nervous."

Julie frowned. "What a rotten way to start your day," she said.

"I nearly forgot—something good happened, too!" I told Amy and Julie about my spider idea.

"I love it," said Amy.

"As long as it's not snakes, I love it too!" said Julie. We all laughed.

"I was thinking we could each learn about a different kind of spider," I said.

"Great idea!" said Julie. "Let's make webs, too."

"Yeah!" agreed Amy. "But won't that be kind of hard?"

"Why don't you come over to my house to do that part?" I said. "My mom's good at art. She'll help us figure out a way to make models of webs."

We hurried into the classroom to write our topic down on the science-fair sign-up sheet. We didn't want anyone else to take our idea!

"Yuck!" said Jessica when she saw what we had written down. "Now I'm double glad I'm not doing the science fair. Spiders give me the creeps!"

"But they're so interesting," said Amy. She had the *S* encyclopedia open on her desk. "Look. Spiders aren't insects. They're—"

"Arachnids," Andy Franklin cut in. He's one of the smartest kids in Mrs. Otis's class. "Everyone knows that."

"Everyone will know everything

about spiders after they see our great exhibit," I said.

"Don't worry about winning any prizes," bragged Andy. "My volcano display is blue-ribbon material!"

"Don't be so sure," I said. "Wait until you see ours. It'll be the very best."

"Kids, I need your attention," called Mrs. Otis. "I'm glad to see everyone so excited about the science fair. But right now we're going to take a math test. Clear your desks, please."

I had studied very hard for this test, so I was finished in a flash. When I turned in my paper, Mrs. Otis asked me to run an errand for her.

"Would you like to go around the school to collect the other science-fair sign-up sheets?"

I liked helping Mrs. Otis, and I felt important going around to all the classrooms. Every class had several students signed up. There would be a lot

14

of displays at the science fair. That would make it more interesting, but harder to win a blue ribbon.

My last stop was Miss Johnson's third-grade class.

"Hello, Elizabeth," said Miss Johnson. "What can I do for you today?"

"I'm collecting the science-fair sign-up sheets for Mrs. Otis," I told her.

Miss Johnson picked the sheet up off her desk and read it over. "Would you mind waiting just a minute?" she asked. "We have a new student who is down in the main office registering for school. Perhaps she would like to sign up, too."

Just then, the classroom door opened. Mrs. Armstrong stepped in with the new student. It was that girl from the bus. She gave me a nasty look, then sat down in the empty desk next to Melanie Mills.

"Patty," asked Miss Johnson, "would you like to participate in the school's

science fair? It's next Friday and it sounds like lots of fun." Miss Johnson gave her the sign-up sheet so she could read the rules.

"I don't like science," Patty said. "I don't want to be in a science fair."

"Are you sure? It might be a good way to get to know other students." Miss Johnson smiled at Patty.

Patty shook her head.

"Thanks for waiting, Elizabeth. Go ahead and take the paper back to Mrs. Otis." Miss Johnson turned around and began writing some long math problems on the board.

I reached for the sign-up sheet. Patty held it out with a smirk. Then she dropped the paper onto the floor. When I bent down to pick it up, she stepped on my fingers. It was no accident! I looked at Miss Johnson. She was still writing on the board.

"Go ahead. Pick it up," whispered Patty.

I rubbed my fingers. They hurt!

"Are you afraid of a piece of paper?" Patty hissed. "What a scaredy-cat."

I used my toe to pull the paper out of reach of her stamping feet. I picked it up off the floor and looked at her. She just laughed her mean laugh.

I always try hard to be friends with everybody. But Patty was pretty hard to like. In one day, she did more mean things than most kids do in a year!

I hurried to Mrs. Otis's classroom. My new high-tops squeaked against the floors in a rhythm that seemed to say "scaredy-cat, scaredy-cat" all the way back.

CHAPTER 3
Jessica Fights Back

The next day started off with Patty in our seat again. She glared at Jessica and me as we walked by.

"We're never going to get our seat back!" Jessica complained.

"I'm starting to like this one," I said. I didn't really mean it, but I didn't want to tangle with Patty again. I was afraid of her.

"She's not very nice," said Jessica.

"I know." I hadn't told Jessica about what had happened in Miss Johnson's class. "Yesterday, she stepped on my fingers on purpose. Then she called me a scaredy-cat." I stared out the window for a minute.

"Do you think I'm a scaredy-cat, Jess?" I asked.

Jessica shook her head. Her ponytail flew back and forth. "No way. That's the *last* thing you are."

I looked out the window again. I had never thought I was a scaredy-cat either. But when Patty smirked at me from our favorite seat, my stomach did the hula. Did that mean I was turning into a scaredy-cat?

Sometimes Jessica can read my mind. "You're the bravest girl I know. You couldn't be a scaredy-cat if you tried." Jessica punched me on the arm.

I punched her back. "Thanks," I said.

"I promise to tell you if you *ever* start doing even the teeniest-tiniest scaredy-cat thing, OK?" Jessica snapped her fingers twice and crossed her heart.

That was our special promise sign.

"OK!" It's great having a twin. Jessica always knew how to cheer me up.

I stayed in a good mood all morning. We did a fun project in art, the spelling test was a cinch, and I got all my math homework right. When it was time for recess, I skipped outside with Jessica, Amy, and Julie.

Melanie Mills ran up to us.

"Elizabeth! I saw what Patty did to you yesterday. That was so mean." Melanie put her hands on her hips.

"Maybe it was an accident," I said. I didn't believe that, but I didn't want to talk about Patty. At all.

Melanie shook her head. "I don't understand why she has to be so mean." Then she shrugged. "There's Crystal. See you guys later." She ran off to play with Crystal Burton.

"Come on, Liz." Jessica grabbed my

21

arm and dragged me over to the hopscotch court. "A good game will take
your mind off Patty."

"For once, hopscotch sounds like
fun," I said. It didn't hurt that the hopscotch area was at the opposite end of
the playground from where Patty was
playing.

"I think I forgot my marker," Amy
said. She fished in her pockets, but
couldn't find it.

"You can borrow my extra one," I
said. I handed Amy a flat black stone
with a white circle around it.

"My mom calls these wishing
stones," said Amy.

We threw our markers to see who
would go first. Amy's stone went far-
thest.

"Looks like my wish came true!"
Amy giggled.

I was last.

I threw my marker, then started to

hop. I had gone two squares when someone came running through our hopscotch game, chasing a ball.

It was Patty. "Oops," she said, shuffling her feet all around. Our markers went flying. "Did I mess up your game? Sorry." She laughed and ran off.

"She did that on purpose!" cried Jessica.

"What is her problem?" asked Amy.

"Come on, you guys," I said. "Let's just try to put the markers back where they were."

We got the game set up again, and I finished my turn. Amy was next, then Julie, then Jessica. Finally, it was my turn again.

I was on one leg, hopping to the next square, when I was hit in the side by a rubber ball. Hard.

"Sorry, Elizabeth," called Patty. I could tell she didn't mean it—she was smiling as if she thought it was funny to hit me.

She grabbed the ball and ran back to the game the big kids were playing.

"You can't let her get away with this!" said Jessica.

"But what can I do?" I asked.

"Tell her to stop," suggested Amy.

Jessica rolled her eyes. "I don't think that would work with Patty."

"Me either," I agreed. "Maybe I should just try to stay away from her. She can't bug me if she can't find me."

"That makes sense," said Julie.

"I don't know," Jessica said. "Patty's mean. I think you should fight back. Treat her the way she treats you, and see how *she* likes it!"

I thought about that. "I think I'll try avoiding her first. It sounds safer."

Mrs. Otis called us to come back inside, so I picked up my hopscotch marker. I took my sister's hand and we skipped toward the school building. The next thing I knew, someone

24

pushed me so hard I nearly fell over.

"Out of my way, scaredy-cat," said Patty.

"You leave her alone!" yelled Jessica.

"Who's going to make me?" asked Patty.

"I am," said Jessica. Her hands were in fists at her sides.

"Oh, I'm scared now. It's a big, mean second-grader!" Patty taunted her. "What are you going to do, second-grader?"

"I'm going to, I'm going to . . ." Jessica was so mad, she had turned all red. "I'm going to . . . tell the playground monitor!"

Patty laughed her mean laugh. She balled *her* hands into fists. "I dare you to tell," said Patty. She waggled her fists in Jessica's face.

I grabbed my sister's hand and we started to run. The last thing I wanted was twin black eyes.

CHAPTER 4

Steven Steps In

The next day, Mrs. Otis gave us some free time after art.

"It's already Thursday," Julie said. "We have just a week and a day until the science fair!"

"You're right," I said. "We've got to decide exactly what we're going to do."

Amy nodded. "What if we each catch a different kind of spider and bring it in a jar for the display?"

"Great idea!" I said. "We could label each jar and write down one or two facts about that kind of spider."

"Don't forget about making webs!" Julie added. "Look, I found this picture in one of my nature magazines." She unrolled the magazine to show us. "It seems like these three webs would be easiest to make."

I read the names of the webs she was pointing to. "Orb web—that's like the one I saw in our tree—triangle web, and common-house-spider web."

"We could put glitter on the webs to make them look like they're covered with dew!" said Amy.

"Neat!" I said with a smile.

"Look at this picture of the wolf spider," said Julie. "I hope I catch one of those!"

Amy leaned over Julie's shoulder. "Oh, wow. A black widow!" She giggled nervously. "I hope I *don't* catch one of those!"

"I never knew there were so many different kinds of spiders," I said. "I like this one—a cross spider." I pointed to the picture of a small orange spider with a tiny silver cross on its back.

Jessica came over to our table. She looked at the book and shivered. "How can twins feel such opposite ways about bugs? I would never, ever want to study spiders."

"Spiders aren't bugs," I explained. "They're—"

"Arachnids," interrupted Jessica. "I know, I know! They're creepy and they're crawly no matter what they're called!" She ran over to talk to Lila.

"Wait until we win the blue ribbon," I said. "Then Jessica will think spiders are wonderful!"

Finally the day was over. Everyone in Mrs. Otis's class got their coats and book bags. Jessica and I gathered our things and headed for the bus line. I was standing there, thinking about spiders, when I felt a tug on my arm.

The next thing I knew, Patty had my book bag.

"Hey, give that back!" I said, reaching for my bag.

She swung it up over my head. "Is this what you want?"

I jumped up to grab it and missed. "Patty, that doesn't belong to you. Give it back."

"Oh, does the scaredy-cat want her book bag?" Patty swung it around and around her head. I knew she was going to let it go and send it flying.

"Cut it out!" I cried.

Patty just laughed.

I leaped at her. She pushed me away with her free hand.

"Knock it off!" It was Steven. "Are you OK, Elizabeth?" he asked.

"I'm not hurt. I just want my book bag back."

Steven turned to face Patty. "The

joke's over. Give that back to Elizabeth right now!"

"I'll give it back to her when I'm ready to," Patty said. She twirled the book bag even harder and hit Caroline Pearce in the face with a strap. Caroline started to cry.

Steven grabbed the book bag and tried to tug it out of Patty's hands. "Give it back!" he yelled.

I was proud of Steven. Patty was much bigger than he was, even though he was older. But he was standing up to her just for me.

Patty gave a hard yank and got the book bag away from Steven. "What are you going to do now, tough guy?" She gave him a mean look. Then she tucked my book bag under one arm and shoved Steven. He fell back against the bus.

He scrambled to his feet and headed straight for Patty.

"Hold it right there!" the bus driver

31

bellowed from the bus door. He frowned at Steven. "What's going on?"

"He's trying to take this away from me," said Patty. She squeezed my book bag tight against her chest.

The bus driver gave Steven a stern look. "Just keep your hands to yourself and leave the other kids alone. In fact, I think you better go to the back of the line."

Steven's mouth was open, but nothing came out. The bus driver pointed. Steven went to the very end of the line. It was so unfair!

The bus driver got back on the bus and motioned for kids to start getting on. I turned to look back at Steven. His shoulders were hunched up and he was staring down at the ground.

Patty saw me looking back. "Here," she said, tossing the book bag at me.

I picked it up and stepped onto the bus. Tears stung my eyes. All because of that rotten Patty. She was such a pain!

CHAPTER 5
A Plan

"Look at this amazing book I found about spiders!" Julie cried, skipping up to me before class the next day.

"Let me see, too!" Amy called.

"Wow! I never knew that some spiders don't spin webs. I thought they all did," I said.

"So did I." Amy read over my shoulder. "It says here that some spiders have *eight* eyes!"

Julie giggled. "It's a good thing they don't have to wear glasses!"

"We should be writing these facts down," I said. "Then we could put them on a poster as part of our display."

Julie grabbed a pencil and a piece of paper. "OK. You read out all the cool stuff."

"Oooh, write this down. Female spiders can lay about a hundred eggs at once!" Amy read.

"This says that the wasp is the spider's worst enemy," I said.

"And water spiders are the only spiders that live most of their life underwater," Amy added.

"Slow down!" interrupted Julie. "I can't write that fast."

Amy giggled. "I never thought I could get excited over spiders."

Mrs. Otis came over. She smiled at us. "I'm glad you girls are having so much fun working on your project! But it's time to start on our spelling lesson now."

When I wrote my name on my spelling paper, I drew a spider over the *i* instead of a dot. I knew Mrs. Otis wouldn't mind.

At recess, Jessica and I ran out to the playground together.

"I finally thought of one good thing about your science project," she said.

"What?"

"Since Halloween is coming up, we can use the spiderwebs you're making for decorations!" Jessica's eyes sparkled. "I want to make our house really scary this year."

"That sounds fun," I said.

"Hey, Elizabeth!" Todd Wilkins called out. "Come play soccer."

I got a ball from the teacher on playground duty and ran over to where Todd and Eva Simpson were playing.

I kicked the ball to Eva. A perfect shot!

But a blur ran across my path, intercepting the ball.

Patty the Pain!

"That's my ball," I shouted at her.

"Not anymore," she called back. She zigzagged across the field. "Bet you can't catch me, scaredy-cat!" I ran after her, but she was fast. Not even Todd or Eva could catch her.

"So much for the soccer game," I said sadly. I flopped onto the grass. Eva sat down next to me.

She put her arm around my shoulder. "Don't let her get to you, Liz. *We* know you're not a scaredy-cat."

Todd nodded. "If she had seen you play goalie against the Smashers, she wouldn't call you that."

"Thanks," I said. Todd and Eva were good friends to try to make me feel better. It wasn't helping, though. It seemed like every time I turned around lately, there was Patty the Pain, calling me names or pushing or poking.

I walked slowly over to where Jessica was jumping rope with Lila and Ellen.

Twins can always tell when something is wrong. I guess that's why Jessica frowned when she saw me.

"What happened?" she asked.

I told her about Patty taking my ball.

"So much for staying away from her," said Jessica. "Now what?"

I just shrugged. I was so unhappy that I didn't even want to talk. Not even the science fair seemed important anymore, not with Patty ruining my life.

"I'm still mad at her for getting Steven into trouble," said Jessica. "Somebody needs to teach Patty a lesson." Jessica squinted her eyes and tapped her toe. I could tell she was trying hard to think of something.

"Jess, I don't think you can help. This is *my* problem. Patty doesn't seem to pick on anyone else."

"Lizzie!" Jessica cried. "Any problem you have is my problem, too. We have to stick together!" She took my hand as Mrs. Otis called us back inside. "Don't worry. We'll think of something to fix Patty the Pain."

All afternoon, Jessica was really quiet in class. She's never quiet! So I knew she must be cooking something up. And during math, Jessica didn't even have her book open to the right page. Her mind was working on a different kind of math problem: How do you subtract a bully from your sister's life?

Right before social studies, Jessica wrote me a note. "I've got it! A brilliant plan."

For once, I couldn't imagine what Jessica was thinking. Sometimes my sister has some pretty crazy ideas. Maybe she really had thought of something to end my Patty problem! I was so excited, I could hardly keep my mind on social studies.

Finally it was time for lunch. Jessica

and I sat together and ate our tuna-fish sandwiches. Tuna fish is our favorite!

"OK," I said, taking a sip of my milk. "What's your great idea?"

Jessica looked over her shoulder as if someone were trying to listen to us. She likes to be mysterious. "It's the perfect plan for putting Patty in her place," she whispered.

"Are you going to call in the Army?" I asked. "I think that's the only thing that could stop Patty the Pain."

"No, but this is just as good." Jessica smiled. "All we need is Julie."

I didn't get it. "Julie? How can she help?"

"You'll see." Jessica smiled mysteriously. "Look, there she is now!"

CHAPTER 6
Karate Kid

Jessica waved to Julie. "I saved you a seat," she called.

Julie brought her lunch and sat next to Jessica. "Hey, Liz, did you know there's a nature show on tonight?" she asked. "Guess what it's about? Spiders!"

"I can't wait! Did you tell Amy?" I asked.

"Not yet." Julie opened her milk carton and took a big sip.

"Maybe you guys can come over to our house. Then we could all watch it together," I suggested.

"Is that all you can talk about?"

Jessica frowned and crossed her arms. "Elizabeth, aren't you even curious about my great plan?"

"What plan?" asked Julie.

Jessica lowered her voice. "I know how Lizzie can get even with that bully Patty!"

"Really? Did you invent some kind of secret weapon?" asked Julie.

Jessica giggled. "Yes. You!"

"Me?" Julie froze with her grilled-cheese sandwich halfway to her mouth. "I'm the secret weapon?"

"Not *you*," explained Jessica. "Your karate lessons! Liz was good at karate in gym class. You just have to teach her some more moves so she can beat Patty up." Jessica smiled proudly and sat back in her chair.

I gulped. "Jess, have you gone crazy? I can't use karate. Even if I was good enough, don't you remember what Mr. Ogata taught us?"

"No," Jessica answered. "I thought karate was boring. *You're* the one who liked it."

"He taught us that real karate is not like what you see in the movies," Julie explained. "You don't go around beating people up." Julie knew a lot about karate. After Mr. Ogata had given us a few lessons at school, Julie had gone on to take more classes. She had been the best karate student in our whole class. "Mr. Ogata says karate is for self-defense only."

Jessica rolled her eyes. "But, Julie, it *is* self-defense. Patty keeps picking on Elizabeth. So Liz has to defend herself. That's self-defense, right?"

Julie shook her head. "I don't think that's what he means. Besides, I haven't been taking lessons long enough to teach anybody else."

I was glad Julie was on my side. I liked karate. But I didn't want to fight anybody. Not even Patty. Especially not Patty.

Jessica thought for a second. "OK, then. *You* beat Patty up," she told Julie.

"I can't do that! Mr. Ogata would be mad if I used karate for fighting." Julie looked very upset. "If there was any way I could help Elizabeth, I would."

Jessica slid down in her chair. She looked discouraged. "It seemed like such a perfect plan," she complained. "Couldn't you give her just a *little* karate chop or something?"

Julie shook her head.

"Jess, be serious," I said. "How many times have Mom and Dad told us that fighting isn't the answer to anything?"

"Well, what is the answer to a big bully?" Jessica asked.

I put my chin in my hands. "I wish I knew."

CHAPTER 7

Sticks and Stones

On Monday morning, I picked out my favorite green sweatshirt to wear. *This will look great with the new four-leaf-clover necklace Grandma and Grandpa Wakefield sent me,* I thought. I opened my jewelry box and pulled out the necklace.

Jessica rolled over in bed to look at me. "Is it time to get up already?" she asked.

"Yes, sleepyhead." I hooked the necklace around my neck.

"That looks nice," she yawned, and rolled back over.

I went downstairs to the kitchen.

"Good morning, honey." Mom set a glass of orange juice on the table for me. "You're up extra early."

"I wanted to finish reading that book on spiders Dad got me," I said. "I got three more facts for our spider poster."

Mom glanced at the calendar next to the phone. "Let's see, the science fair is this Friday, isn't it?"

"Yup. Just five more days. I can't wait!" I buttered my toast.

"You and Amy and Julie have been working very hard on your exhibit. You should be proud of yourselves." Mom leaned over and kissed my forehead.

"Can Amy and Julie come over after school this week to work on webs?" I asked.

"Hmmm. Tomorrow won't work because of dance lessons. How about Wednesday?" said Mom.

"Great. I'll tell them today."

*   *   *

I hadn't seen Patty the Pain all weekend. I was hoping she had forgotten about making fun of me. But when we got on the bus, there was Patty, sitting in our seat.

"Let's sit here today," said Jessica. I followed her to the back of the bus.

"Good morning, Elizabeth," Patty sang as I walked down the aisle. "Or should I call you scaredy-cat?" As I passed Patty, I felt a sharp tug at the back of my head. She had pulled on my ponytail! I just kept walking.

"Scaredy-cat," she repeated.

My eyes were watering as I slid into the seat next to Jessica.

"Why doesn't she leave you alone?" Jessica whispered.

I sniffled. Things were getting worse and worse with Patty. She went out of her way to make me miserable. I'd had my ponytail pulled, my book bag dumped out, and my homework crumpled. I'd been tripped, pushed, pulled, and even stepped on! I felt like a puppet with its strings all twisted.

When we got to school, Amy met me as I climbed off the bus.

"I forgot to give this back to you," she said. "But with Patty around, I think you need it." She handed me a small black rock.

"My wishing rock?" I said.

"Maybe you could wish that she'd turn into a frog and hop away," Amy suggested. "Or that she'd move to Alaska."

I held the rock in my hand. "I wish—"

"Stop, don't tell me! Then it won't come true." Amy covered her ears.

I grinned. "OK, I won't tell you. Even though you already know."

Amy giggled.

"And if the wishing rock doesn't work, this might." I showed Amy my new necklace.

"A four-leaf clover! That should bring double luck," said Amy.

I nodded. "Grandma and Grandpa sent Jessica a unicorn. It's pretty, but I'd rather have this, for luck."

"I don't blame you." Amy looked thoughtful. "Do you think things like wishes and four-leaf clovers really work?"

"I'm not sure," I answered. "But as long as Patty's around, I need all the help I can get. Is Julie here yet?"

Amy shrugged. "Let's go find out," she said.

Inside our classroom, we saw Julie standing near Mrs. Otis's desk. She was holding a big plastic jar and wearing a huge smile.

"Guess what I've got in here," she called to us.

"A spider!" Amy and I guessed together.

"I never thought I would be so happy

about a spider," I said. We all giggled.

"It's not any old spider," Julie said, sounding excited. "It's a wolf spider. Just what I wanted for our display." She held up the jar so we could see.

"I keep forgetting to catch my spider," said Amy.

"I haven't done that, either," I said. "We better get busy."

"Can you believe it?" asked Julie. "Only four more days until the science fair. I can hardly wait!"

"I can't wait until we get that blue ribbon," I said.

"We still have to make the webs," Amy reminded me.

"I know. That's the most important part!" I said. "Can you guys come over Wednesday after school?"

Amy and Julie said they'd ask their moms. Then we went to our seats. Julie carried her spider very carefully. She put him on the windowsill by the pencil sharpener. All morning, kids kept sharpening their pencils! They all made sure to take a long time, so they could watch Julie's spider. Jessica made a face whenever someone went near the jar. She wouldn't even go near the windowsill!

When it was lunchtime, Amy, Julie, Jessica, and I walked to the cafeteria together.

"Did you know a female tarantula can lay up to four thousand eggs?" Julie asked. She was looking in a new nature magazine.

"Ugh! Don't read any more," begged Jessica. "Spiders are not what I want to talk about at lunch!"

"Jess, you look a little green!" I teased her. "I better not tell you what I learned about how spiders eat."

Jessica sniffed. "I'm going to sit with Lila and Ellen. They talk about normal things!"

Julie and I had brought lunch, but we waited in line to buy milk.

"Dad got the neatest book on spiders at the library," I told Julie. "The pictures are so—ouch!"

Someone's sharp elbow bashed me right in my ribs. I rubbed my side and looked around. Patty the Pain!

She elbowed a few other people and barged to the front of the line.

"Hey, no cutting," called Charlie Cashman.

"She was saving me a place," Patty said. She pointed to Lois Waller.

"No, I wasn't," said Lois.

"Yes, you were," Patty growled.

Lois bit her lip. "It's against the rules to let you cut," she said quietly.

"What are you going to do about it?" asked Patty.

Lois looked as if she wished she could disappear. She sniffled loudly.

"You're so fat, you don't even need to

eat lunch," Patty said. "Maybe I'll eat your food instead." She grabbed the cookie off Lois's tray.

Lois started to cry. Patty had gone too far. Lois was a little chubby and she cried a lot, but she was my friend. No one gets away with being mean to my friends. I marched over to Patty.

"Give Lois the cookie," I said.

"Are you going to make me?" asked Patty.

I thought for a minute. I didn't know what to say. I tried to keep calm.

"You're never going to make friends here if you keep acting like this," I said. I looked Patty right in the eyes.

"I don't care what you think, shrimp." Patty dropped Lois's cookie into the nearest trash can.

"Why are you so mean to people?" I shouted. I couldn't keep calm anymore. "You're a big bully!" My cheeks felt hot. Everyone was staring at me.

Patty's hands tightened into fists. "Sticks and stones can break my bones, but names will never hurt me," she sang. Then she grabbed the front of my sweatshirt.

"Let go," I yelled, and jerked away. I didn't realize Patty had ahold of my necklace, too. The chain snapped. The four-leaf-clover charm bounced on the floor.

"My new necklace!" Now *I* felt like crying. I could feel the tears in my eyes.

Patty got a funny look on her face for a second, as if she might cry, too. Then her mean look came back. "You're not just a scaredy-cat, you're a crybaby, too!" she said. She turned and ran out of the cafeteria, knocking into kids as she passed them.

I picked up the pieces of my chain and the little gold four-leaf clover. I guess with Patty around, nothing could bring me good luck.

CHAPTER 8

Parents to the Rescue

"I can't decide what to wear," Jessica complained on Wednesday morning. She held up her pink sweatshirt with the unicorn on it.

"That looks nice," I said.

"It will look perfect with the new unicorn necklace Grandma and Grandpa Wakefield gave me," she said, rummaging in her "special things" box. Then she gasped. "Oh, I'm sorry, Lizzie! I forgot." She closed her box. "I won't wear my necklace, since you can't wear yours."

I picked up the four-leaf clover off

my dresser. It had been such a pretty necklace. I sighed.

"You should wear your necklace, Jess. It *will* look great with that shirt," I said.

"You're sure it won't bother you?" she asked.

"Well, I'm sad that my necklace is broken, but I'd feel even worse if you didn't wear yours because of me." I put my broken necklace back on my dresser and handed Jessica her "special things" box. "Go on, wear it."

"It does look nice, doesn't it?" Jessica said as she put the necklace on. "Maybe we could take turns wearing this one," she suggested.

"Thanks," I said, "but I don't like unicorns that much. I just won't have a necklace." I noticed that my sister was frowning at me, so I tried to look happy. "Don't worry about me," I told her as we headed downstairs.

But I could tell Jessica *was* worried about me. She tried to get me to laugh—or at least smile—on the bus to school. Nothing cheered me up. Not Jessica's silly stories or the big sign on the blackboard that said TWO DAYS TO THE SCIENCE FAIR. Not even Todd's new knock-knock joke book. Not anything.

Julie set a huge bag on my desk. "I brought some stuff for making webs. Yarn and glitter and things."

I peeked in the bag. "This looks great!" I tried to smile at Julie. But it wasn't a real smile.

One good thing happened that day, though. Patty didn't ride the bus home. She must have had a dentist appointment or something. Whatever it was, I wasn't complaining. Jessica, Julie, Amy, and I all squeezed together on one seat. It was the best bus ride I'd had since Patty moved to Sweet Valley.

Mom was waiting for us when we got

home. She asked Jessica to fix us all a snack (she made *her* favorite, cinnamon-raisin toast). Then Jessica went off to play with her stuffed animals. She didn't want anything to do with the spider project.

Mom looked at the supplies Julie had brought. "This is wonderful," she said. Mom had found some other things for us, too. There was sparkly white yarn, nice big pieces of cardboard, and a new box of colored markers. We got to work. We used up almost a whole bottle of glue before we got the webs just how we wanted them!

"Amy, the glitter makes the webs look so real. What a good idea!" said Mom.

Amy looked proud. "Thanks, Mrs. Wakefield."

We all stood back and admired the three webs. They were perfect—as if real spiders had made them. But the sparkly strands reminded me of my broken necklace.

"This calls for a celebration!" said Mom. We went into the kitchen, and Mom made hot cocoa topped with real whipped cream. Amy and Julie talked about spiders while we drank, but all I could think of was bullies.

"Elizabeth, you're not drinking your cocoa," said Mom.

"I don't feel like any right now, Mom," I said.

Jessica wandered into the kitchen. "Mmm. That smells good!" she said. "Can I have some?"

"Here, I'm not going to drink this. You can have it." I gave my cup to Jessica.

She took a sip. "I saw your spider-webs in the other room. They look real!"

"Do you like them?" asked Julie.

Jessica grinned. "I just know you'll

60

win the blue ribbon," she said. "Are you guys finished with the webs?"

I nodded.

"Then do you want to play charades?" asked Jessica.

"Yes!" shouted Amy and Julie together. We played charades until Mrs. Sutton came to pick up Julie and Amy.

At dinner, Mom and Jessica told Dad about our spiderwebs.

"I can't wait to see your display all set up, Elizabeth," said Dad. "How about some more fruit salad?" Dad held the salad bowl out to me. "It's your favorite!"

I shook my head. "No, thanks."

Mom put down her fork. "You've hardly touched any of your dinner. Don't you feel well?"

I shrugged. "I guess I'm just not very hungry."

Mom frowned. "You've been awfully quiet all afternoon."

Dad looked at Jessica. She looked down at her plate. Steven was studying his green beans very intently.

"OK. Something's up here," he said. "And I think it's time we were in on it."

Mom looked at each one of us.

Jessica and Steven both turned to me.

"Elizabeth?" Mom asked.

I took a deep breath. Then I told them all about Patty the Pain, from the first day on the bus to yesterday with Lois and the cookie. I told them everything. Well, *almost* everything. I don't know why, but I didn't tell them about my necklace. I just couldn't.

"I'm very proud of you for standing up to that bully and for sticking up for Lois," said Dad.

"And it shows that you're growing up when you try to solve your problems for yourself," added Mom. "But it sounds like it's time to involve some adults. Perhaps I should call Patty's parents."

"And I think we should let Mrs. Armstrong know what's going on," said Dad.

"No! Please don't," I said. I knew what would happen if Mom or Dad made any phone calls. Patty would call me a scaredy-cat—or worse.

"Wait a few more days before you call anyone," I asked. "I *know* I'm no scaredy-cat. And I'll find a way to prove it to Patty the Pain."

CHAPTER 9

Patty's Sad Secret

Julie was waiting for us as Amy and I walked into the classroom the next day.

"Where are the jars?" she asked.

"What jars?" I asked.

"Your spider jars!" Julie pointed to the calendar. "We only have until tomorrow."

"We'll get them," I said. "Don't worry."

"When? Time is running out!" Julie's eyes were big.

"I know," I said. "Amy and I can go spider hunting at recess. There are millions of spiders running around out there."

"Don't say that!" said Jessica from her desk. "That gives me the creeps."

"You two have to catch spiders today," said Julie seriously. "It's the last chance."

Mrs. Otis keeps extra empty jars in the classroom. "I'm happy to lend these to you for your project," she said. Amy and I each got a jar with a lid out of the closet and put them on our desks.

As soon as recess started, Amy and I hurried out to go spider hunting.

"I'm going to look over there, under the office windows," said Amy. "Spiders like to hide around windows."

"Good idea." I looked around the playground. "I'll go over there, by those bushes."

"Happy hunting!" Amy called back to me.

I wandered off by myself, snooping

around under shrubs and other nice dry places spiders would like.

There's a gigantic bush at the edge of the playground that everyone is afraid of. It's so big that you can crawl *inside* it! Lila says it looks like a witch's lair. I decided to check it out. It would be the perfect place to find spiders. Besides, I'm no scaredy-cat. I'm not afraid of a creepy-looking bush.

It was dark and cold under the bush. But it wasn't too scary. No one could see me in there, so it was kind of like a fort. But there were no spiders. Not one!

As I started to climb out, I heard a funny noise. Maybe the bush *was* haunted! I peeked out between the branches. Someone was sitting all alone by the playground wall. It was Patty the Pain. She was crying.

I crawled all the way out and tried to sneak away, but she saw me.

"Are you spying on me?" Patty quickly wiped her eyes.

"No. I'm just looking for something for my science project." I took a few steps toward her. "Are you OK?"

Patty sniffled. "I'm fine." She crossed her arms over her chest.

"Do you want me to get Miss Johnson?" I asked. I wondered why Patty was all by herself and why she was crying. I remembered that I hardly ever saw her playing with any of the other kids from Miss Johnson's class—or any other class.

"No, I want you to go away." She was trying to sound mean, but there was too much sadness in her voice.

"Is something wrong?" I asked.

"What could be wrong?" Patty said sharply. "Just because my mom left me here with my grandma while she started a new job in Oregon, that doesn't mean anything's wrong." Patty stared at her shoes. "Things are just perfect."

I was surprised. Jessica and I had been at Sweet Valley Elementary for a long time—ever since kindergarten! We'd never had to move or make all new friends. I wondered if Patty was lonely. I'd never thought about that before.

Patty's eyes were still watery. I felt sorry for her. "You miss your mom, don't you?" I asked softly.

Patty got that funny look on her face. Then she exploded. "Why don't you just mind your own business?" She shoved me aside and ran away.

I guess Patty doesn't know how to be anything but a pain.

CHAPTER 10

Science Superstars

I woke up. For a second I couldn't remember why I felt so wiggly. Then I jumped out of bed. "Wake up, sleepyhead, it's Friday!" I shook Jessica awake.

"Elizabeth," she grumbled. "What's the big deal?"

"It's the day of the science fair!" I bounced on her bed. The big day had finally arrived! Our spider display was all set. We each had a spider in a jar to bring. Dad had helped me catch a trapdoor spider. Julie had her wolf spider, and Amy had found a house spider.

Everything about our display was perfect, from the poster to the webs. Even Steven was impressed.

Jessica rubbed her eyes. "I hope you win the blue ribbon," she said. "But that won't change how I feel about spiders!"

I hurried down to breakfast and gave Mom a big hug. "I'm so excited!" I told her.

She smiled. "I thought I'd drive you to school today. It might be kind of tricky to get those webs and your spider to school safely on the bus."

"Mom, you're the greatest!" I gave her another hug. "Today is going to be terrific! Even if we don't win the blue ribbon."

Amy and Julie were waiting for me at school.

I hopped out of the car. "Here, Jess. Help me." I handed her my spider jar.

"No way!" Jessica shuddered. "I'll

carry the webs. They don't crawl!"

We all hurried to the gym to get set up. It was very noisy, and kids were bustling around everywhere.

"Where's my vinegar?" called Andy Franklin. He was pawing through some bags in front of his display. "I found the baking soda, but where's the vinegar?" He bent over to look under the table. "I know it's here somewhere," he mumbled.

Julie pointed to a bottle on a nearby table. "Is that it?" she asked.

"Whew!" Andy grabbed the bottle. "My volcano would be a dud without this. Thanks."

Todd and Kisho stood by our table for a minute. "You did a good job on that poster," said Kisho.

"The webs are neat, too," said Todd. "But wait until you see our tornado tube!" They walked over to set up their project.

"You know something?" said Amy. "Kisho, Todd, and Andy are the only other second-graders who have displays."

"That makes us *extra* special," said Julie.

Mrs. Armstrong peeked her head in the gym.

"My, this is certainly a colorful and lively exhibit," she said as she stopped by our table. Amy and Julie were arranging branches and leaves around the spider jars. I was hanging the spiderwebs. "It's obvious that you worked very hard on this," she added.

"We did!" I said.

"Great job!" Mrs. Armstrong gave us a thumbs-up before moving on to check on the other displays. I felt as if I were floating on a cloud.

Andy had finished setting up his volcano. He came over and watched our spiders for a while. "Can I have these guys when you're done?" he asked.

"No way!" said Julie. Amy and I shook our heads too.

"We're going to put them back where we found them," I explained. "It wouldn't be fair to take them away from their real homes forever."

"Besides, I don't want to have to catch any more flies for food," said Amy. "That's the worst part of this whole project."

Julie and I agreed.

"Your spiders *are* very interesting," admitted Andy. "Nearly as interesting as my volcano." He wasn't bragging, just teasing.

Julie arranged the last of the leaves and then brushed her hands. "We're almost finished."

"We have to hang the poster, and that should be it," I said.

Just then Mrs. Otis blew a whistle. "Time to get to class," she said. "You can come back at lunchtime to finish setting up."

"I wish we could stay in here all day," said Amy.

"Me, too," I said. "I could work on our display for hours."

"And I'd like to look at the other exhibits before the crowds come," added Julie.

"I want to stay so we don't have to take our math test!" Amy said.

I laughed. We went back to class and did our regular class work, plus our math test. Finally, it was lunchtime and we could get back to our exhibit.

The three of us rushed to the gym.

"Oh, no!" said Julie. She stopped and pointed.

I looked where she was pointing. There, standing right by our exhibit, was Patty the Pain.

CHAPTER 11

Patty Panics

"What are you doing?" I ran up to Patty, frantically looking to see if anything was missing.

Patty just stood there. For once, she didn't have any smart-aleck reply. She didn't say a word. She didn't move a muscle, either. She was like a statue.

"What are you doing?" I asked again.

She moved her lips just a little. "Sssppider," she whispered. "There's a spider on me."

"Oh, no!" cried Amy. "I didn't put the lid on tight." Her spider had

escaped from its jar and was crawling up Patty's arm.

"It's not poisonous or anything," I told Patty.

"Get—it—off—me!" Patty hardly moved her lips to talk.

For a minute, I was tempted to let that spider crawl all the way up her arm. Maybe even into her hair. "Why should I?"

"Please get it off me!" Patty begged.

I looked at her. "Who's the scaredy-cat now?"

Patty watched the spider crawl slowly up her arm. She started to cry.

For a second, I was glad. She had been so mean to me. At last I'd found some way to get back at her. But when I saw her teary eyes, I realized that just because she'd been mean to me was no reason to be mean back.

"Hold still," I said to Patty. "Amy, hand me your jar." I scooped up Amy's spider and carefully dropped it back into its jar.

"I'll put the lid on tight this time," said Amy.

Patty turned to look at me. "I suppose you're going to tell everyone what a baby I am about spiders."

I thought about what she'd said to me the day before, when I'd found her crying. "No, I won't tell," I said. I snapped my fingers twice and crossed my heart. "And that's a Wakefield promise!"

Patty's eyes got big. "You won't? Not even after how I've treated you?"

I shook my head. Right now, Patty didn't look as if she could hurt a fly. "Now that you know how it feels to be called a scaredy-cat, maybe you won't do it anymore."

"How come you're being so nice to me?" Patty asked suspiciously.

"Because I think it must be hard to

move to a new school and have to make all new friends."

Patty nodded. "It is hard."

"Maybe I could help," I suggested. "Then you wouldn't be so lonely. Would you like to play soccer with Todd and Eva and some other kids on Monday?"

Patty blinked. "I'm pretty good at soccer."

"I know you are!" I smiled, remembering how fast she'd run the day when she'd taken my ball. "But so are we. We'll have fun, I promise. And you'll meet some more kids, too."

Patty was quiet for a second. "Thanks. I'd like that." Then she stuck out her hand. "Anybody who can touch a spider is no scaredy-cat. You are no scaredy-cat, Elizabeth Wakefield."

"And neither are you, Patty . . . Hey, I don't know your last name!" I said.

She grinned. "It's Payne. Patty Payne."

CHAPTER 12
A New Friend—Sort Of

"We won!" I ran up to our exhibit as soon as I saw the blue ribbon. My family was right behind me.

"Isn't it great?" Amy and Julie came over too. "Look, it's for 'Most Realistic Exhibit.'"

"I'm so happy, I could jump as high as a jumping spider!" I said.

"Can I take a picture before you jump too far?" asked Dad.

Amy, Julie, and I wrapped our arms around each other and smiled huge smiles.

Then I showed my family around the whole gym.

"What wonderful displays!" said Mom.

"I feel like I'm in a museum," Dad added.

"I'm so tired of science-fair this and science-fair that," complained Jessica. "I can't wait until we start to decorate the gym for Halloween! I want to have the spookiest Halloween ever!"

"We've already got a good start, with these spiderwebs," I said.

Jessica nodded. "But I want to make it even more scary. Maybe have a haunted house or something. Maybe—"

"Uh-oh." I laughed. "Watch out! Jessica's cooking up something extra-special spooky for Halloween."

"Speaking of Halloween," said Dad, "what's the first thing vampires learn in school?"

"What?" asked Jessica.

"The alpha-*bat*," answered Dad. We all laughed.

Steven came hurrying up. "Come on, you guys," he said. "It's time for Andy's volcano to go off!"

We got there just as Andy's volcano bubbled out its vinegar and soda foam. Andy had added red food coloring, so it really looked like lava erupting.

"Maybe science isn't so boring, after all," said Jessica.

"It's not boring," I said. "It's cool!"

Dad took one last picture of the three of us with our blue ribbon.

"That'll be a great picture," said Mrs. Otis. She smiled at us. "Congratulations on the blue ribbon, girls."

"You should get a blue ribbon, too," I said. "For putting on the best science fair ever."

"I'd settle for some help putting away chairs," Mrs. Otis answered.

"I think that's my cue," said Dad. He

handed Mom the camera. "Put me to work!" Dad followed Mrs. Otis to the other side of the gym.

"The gym will look so bare after all the displays are gone," said Mom.

"Not for long," said Jessica. "Just wait until—"

"I know, wait until it gets decorated for Halloween! You're beginning to sound like a broken record," I teased Jessica.

"It's late. We'd better take the display down," said Mom. "You can help, Jessica." Mom gave her a box. Jessica made a face.

"I like putting things up better than taking them down," she grumbled.

Amy picked up her spider jar. She tapped gently on the glass. "It's almost time for you to go home, Mr. Spider."

Julie peeked into her jar. "I'm going to miss our eight-legged friends," she said.

"Me, too." I looked at my little spider.

"But think how happy they'll be to get back to their real homes."

I was taking down one of the spider-webs when I heard someone call my name.

It was Patty the P— I mean, Patty Payne.

"You had a good exhibit," Patty said. "Even if it was about spiders!" We both smiled.

All around us, moms and dads were taking down tables and sweeping up the gym. Andy had his volcano packed away. Kisho and Todd had already gone home.

"Don't forget this," Patty said, handing me a small box.

"What is it?" I asked.

"Look and see."

I opened the box. Inside was a delicate gold chain. Just right for my four-leaf-clover charm. "Thanks, Patty." I guess that four-leaf clover brought me luck, after all.

"We're finished," said Amy.

"Now we have to carry everything back out to the car," I said.

"I can help," said Patty. She picked up the nearest box. "Lead the way."

When we got to the car, Dad helped us load things carefully so nothing would get crushed or broken.

"Thanks for your help, Patty," I said.

"I liked helping," she said. She stood there for a moment longer. "I was wondering something," she said finally.

"Wondering what?" I asked.

"You're so good at this kind of thing"—she touched the spiderwebs we'd made—"I wondered if you could come over and help me decorate my grandma's house for Halloween."

"Sure! We could even make some of these spiderwebs," I said. "They're easy. We could also make construction-paper bats and tissue-paper ghosts."

Jessica had been listening. "We won't

need to do much decorating at *our* house for Halloween," she said mysteriously. "Not when we've got our own ghost."

*Do the Wakefields really live in a haunted house? Find out in Sweet Valley Kids #62, **THE HALLOWEEN WAR.***

SIGN UP FOR THE SWEET VALLEY HIGH® FAN CLUB!

Hey, girls! Get all the gossip on Sweet Valley High's® most popular teenagers when you join our fantastic Fan Club! As a member, you'll get all of this really cool stuff:

- Membership Card with your own personal Fan Club ID number
- A Sweet Valley High® Secret Treasure Box
- Sweet Valley High® Stationery
- Official Fan Club Pencil (for secret note writing!)
- Three Bookmarks
- A "Members Only" Door Hanger
- Two Skeins of J. & P. Coats® Embroidery Floss with flower barrette instruction leaflet
- Two editions of *The Oracle* newsletter
- Plus exclusive Sweet Valley High® product offers, special savings, contests, and much more!

Be the first to find out what Jessica & Elizabeth Wakefield are up to by joining the Sweet Valley High® Fan Club for the one-year membership fee of only $6.25 each for U.S. residents, $8.25 for Canadian residents (U.S. currency). Includes shipping & handling.

Send a check or money order (do not send cash) made payable to "Sweet Valley High® Fan Club" along with this form to:

SWEET VALLEY HIGH® FAN CLUB, BOX 3919-B, SCHAUMBURG, IL 60168-3919

NAME_____
(Please print clearly)

ADDRESS_____

CITY_____ STATE _____ ZIP_____
(Required)

AGE_____ BIRTHDAY_____ /_____ /_____

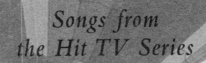
*Songs from
the Hit TV Series*

Featuring:

"*Rose Colored
Glasses*"

"*Lotion*"

"*Sweet Valley High
Theme*"

*Available on CD and Cassette
Wherever Music is Sold.*